Be My Valentine

Text and jacket art by

Rosemary Wells

Interior illustrations by

John Nez

Hyperion Books for Children
New York

Copyright © 2001 by Rosemary Wells
Volo and the Volo colophon are trademarks of Disney Enterprises, Inc.
All rights reserved. No part of this book may be reproduced or transmitted in
any form or by any means, electronic or mechanical, including photocopying,
recording, or by any information storage and retrieval system, without written
permission from the publisher. For information address
Hyperion Books for Children, 114 Fifth Avenue,
New York, New York 10011-5690.

Printed in the United States of America
First Edition
3 5 7 9 10 8 6 4

LIBRARY OF CONGRESS CATALOGING-IN-PUBLICATION DATA
Wells, Rosemary.
Be my valentine / Rosemary Wells.—1st ed.
p. cm. — (Yoko and friends—school days)
Summary: Confusion arises as Yoko's classmates secretly trade Valentine's Day cards.
ISBN 0-7868-0724-5 (hc.)—ISBN 0-7868-1530-2 (pbk.)
[1. Valentine's Day—Fiction. 2. Schools—Fiction. 3. Animals—Fiction.]
I. Title.
PZ7.W46843 Bd 2001
[E]—dc21
00-49905
Visit www.hyperionchildrensbooks.com

Timothy got on the school bus.

He did not sit next to Yoko.

Timothy had a secret valentine

for Yoko.

3

He had made it out of red silk
and a white lace paper doily with
candy hearts.

Timothy's mother had wrapped
the valentine carefully.

Timothy was afraid Yoko might
not like his valentine best. He was
afraid she might hate candy hearts.

"Why aren't you sitting next to

Yoko?" asked Charles.

"Because," said Timothy.

"What's that funny-looking thing

in your book bag?" asked Charles.

"Nothing," said Timothy.

"Well, I brought a secret

valentine," said Charles.

"You did?" asked Timothy.

"Oh, yes," said Charles. "I put

red-hot zingers and fruity zappers

on my secret valentine, but she

will never guess who it is from."

"You must be so scared to tell

her," said Timothy.

"Oh, yes," said Charles.

"Me, too," said Timothy.

"Who is yours for?" asked Charles.

"Yoko!" Timothy whispered.

"Who is yours for?"

"Lily," said Charles.

"Lily's easy," said Timothy.

"She likes everything

and everyone."

Lily and Yoko sat next to each

other on the bus.

Lily spotted a big envelope

sticking out of Yoko's bag.

"What is that thing in there?"

asked Lily.

Yoko whispered, "My valentine for Timothy—but I didn't sign my name on it, because I don't know if he'll like it!"

"Oh, no!" said Lily.

"What?" asked Yoko.

"I forgot my special valentine!"

"Who was it for?" asked Yoko.

"Charles," whispered Lily.

"Don't worry," said Yoko.

"We have all morning to make

another—Mrs. Jenkins said we

could make them in class.

You can use some of

my special Japanese candy."

"We are going to make valentines this morning, boys and girls," said Mrs. Jenkins. "Be sure you make a valentine for everyone. Why is that, boys and girls?"

"So everybody is happy," said everyone.

"And no one's feelings are hurt,"
said Mrs. Jenkins.
"When we are finished, we will
put the valentines in each person's
cubby."

Timothy whispered to Charles:

"Will you take my valentine for

Yoko so she doesn't see me

putting it in her cubby?"

"Yes," said Charles.

"I'll do the same with your

valentine for Lily," said Timothy.

Timothy said to Charles, "Oh!

I know someone we forgot!"

"You do?" said Charles.

"Yes. We need to make another

valentine right away!"

said Timothy.

Charles and Timothy cut out red

paper hearts. They pasted them

onto special paper.

"This will really be a surprise,"

said Charles.

Yoko took out her lunch.

For dessert, her mother had given

her Mount Fuji drops.

Yoko gave some to Lily.

"They erupt in your mouth, just like a volcano," said Yoko.

"Take some for Charles's valentine."

Lily drew trucks all over Charles's
valentine.

She sprinkled gold glitter on it
and glued the Japanese candy to
the edges.

"Will you please put the
valentines in the cubbies, Lily?"
Yoko asked.

"Of course," said Lily.

Lily stood in front of the cubbies. "I can't really read yet," she whispered. "I wonder which one says *Charles*? What letter does *Charles* begin with? Any one of them could say *Charles*."

Lily looked at all the names on the
cubbies. "I think this is the right
one," she said.

"Yoko, take this," said Charles.

"It's super secret!"

"Oh," said Yoko.

She added Mount Fuji drops to the secret valentine. Lily added some glitter.

"This is a wonderful surprise!" said Yoko.

Charles opened his valentine.

"Trucks and gold glitter!" he said.

"I love trucks! This must be

from Lily!"

Yoko opened her valentine. "Oh,"
she said. "Red silk and white lace!
How pretty! This must be from
Timothy!"

Timothy opened his valentine.

"An origami paper heart!

This must be from Yoko!

I'm so happy!"

Lily opened hers.

"Oh, red–hot zingers! I know this

must be from Charles!" said Lily.

"I love trucks!" said Charles.

"I know!" said Lily.

"That's why I drew trucks

on yours!"

"And I love candy hearts!"

said Yoko.

"Thank heavens!" said Timothy.

Lily looked at the card with the

red-hot zingers and said,

"Zingers are my favorite!"

"I am so glad!" said Charles.

26

"Does everyone have all their valentines?" asked Mrs. Jenkins.

"Yes, Mrs. Jenkins," answered the whole class.

"That's strange. There's one valentine here," said Mrs. Jenkins. "There's no name on it."

"Open it," said the class.

So Mrs. Jenkins opened it.

"Why, it's for me,"

said Mrs. Jenkins.

"Origami paper, Mount Fuji

drops, candy hearts, and glitter!

All my favorite things," said

Mrs. Jenkins.

"Happy Valentine's Day,
Mrs. Jenkins!" said the class.
"And Happy Valentine's Day to
you!" said Mrs. Jenkins.

On the school bus home,

Timothy sat next to Yoko.

Timothy took off his sweater.

"You have pinned my origami

heart to your pocket!" said Yoko.

"It is the most beautiful heart I

have ever seen," said Timothy.

"Timothy, you didn't have to

worry," said Yoko.

"No matter what kind of candy

you glue on, it's the thought

behind the valentine that counts!

Would you like a Mount Fuji drop?"

"I'll trade you for a candy heart!"

said Timothy.

Dear Parents,

When our children were young we lived in a small house, but we always made a space just for books. When their dad or I would read a story out loud, the TV was always off—radio and music, too—because it intruded.

Soon this peaceful half hour of every day became like a little island vacation. Our children are lifetime readers now, with an endless curiosity for the rich world waiting between the covers of good books. It cost us nothing but time well spent and a library card.

This set of easy-to-read books is about the real nitty-gritty of elementary school. There are new friends, and bullies, too. There are germs and the "Clean Hands" song, new ways of painting pictures, learning music, telling the truth, gossiping, teasing, laughing, crying, separating from Mama, scary Halloweens, and secret valentines. The stories are all drawn from the experiences my children had in school.

It's my hope that these books will transport you and your children to a setting that's familiar, yet new, a place where you can explore the exciting new world of school together.

Rosemary Wells